DISASTER ALERT!

TERRORISM ALERT!

Lynn Peppas and Sydney Newton

Crabtree Publishing Company
www.crabtreebooks.com

DISASTER ALERT!

presented by:

Crabtree Publishing Company

www.crabtreebooks.com

Coordinating editor: Ellen Rodger
Project editors: Ellen Rodger and L. Michelle Nielsen
Editors: Rachel Eagen, Carrie Gleason
Book design and production coordinator: Rosie Gowsell
Production assistant: Samara Parent
Scanning technician: Arlene Arch-Wilson
Art Director: Rob MacGregor
Photo research: Allison Napier
Consultant: Dr. Paul Hamilton, Political Science, Brock University

Photographs: AP/ Wide World Photos: p. 4, p. 12 (top); Bibliotheque Nationale, Paris, France, Archives Charmet/ Bridgeman Art Library: p. 8; Bibliotheque Nationale, Paris, France/ Bridgeman Art Library: p. 5 (bottom); Musee de la Ville de Paris, Musee Carnavalet, Paris, France, Lauros / Giraudon/ Bridgeman Art Library: p. 9; Museo e Gallerie Nazionali di Capodimonte, Naples, Italy/ Bridgeman Art Library: p. 6; Lynsey Addario/ Corbis Saba: p. 25 (bottom); Bettmann/ Corbis: p. 3, p. 7, p. 10, p. 12 (bottom), p. 15, p. 18 (top), p. 21 (both), p. 22 (bottom), p. 23 (bottom); Andy Clark/ Reuters/ Corbis: p. 28; Corbis: p. 22 (top); Neville Elder/ Corbis: p. 5 (top); Sysoyev Grigory/ ITAR-TASS/ Corbis: p. 26; Shaun Heasley/ Reuters/ Corbis: p. 30 (bottom); Ralf-Finn Hestoft/ Corbis: p. 1; Hulton-Deutsch Collection/ Corbis: p. 20; Reinhard Krause/ Reuters/ Corbis: p. 31; JP Laffont/ Sygma/ Corbis: p. 25 (top); Danny Lehman/ Corbis: p. 30 (top); Catherine Leuthold/ Corbis: p. 29; Alain Nogues/ Corbis Sygma: p. 13; Thierry Orban/ Corbis Sygma: p. 17; p. Perrin/ Corbis Sygma: p. 11 (bottom); Reuters/ Corbis: p. 14, p. 19, p. 24; Jeffrey L. Rotman/ Corbis: p. 16 (top right); David Rubinger/ Corbis: p. 27 (bottom); Yomiuri Shibun/ Corbis Sygma: p. 27 (top); Greg Smith/ Corbis: p. 16 (bottom); Steve Starr/ Corbis: p. 11 (top); STR/ AFP/ Getty Images: p. 23 (top); Kael Alford/ Panos Pictures: p. 18 (bottom); Ken Cavanagh/ Photo Researchers Inc.: cover. Other images form cd stock.

Cover: On September 11, 2001, terrorists hijacked four airplanes, two of which they flew into the World Trade Center in New York. The other planes were crashed into the Pentagon and went down in a Pennsylvania field. In return, the United States and some other governments of the world, including Great Britain, declared a "War on Terror."

Contents: On September 6, 1970, the Popular Front for the Liberation of Palestine, or PFLP, hijacked three planes. They took the passengers hostage, wanting their people freed from jail in return for the release of the passengers. The hijacked planes burned in the desert in Jordan, in the Middle East.

Title page: On April 19, 1995, a truck bomb exploded in front of the Federal Building in Oklahoma City, Oklahoma. Rescue workers searched the remains of the building for survivors.The terrorist attack killed 168 people.

Crabtree Publishing Company
www.crabtreebooks.com 1-800-387-7650

 In Canada: We acknowledge the financial support of the Government of Canada through the Canada Book Fund for our publishing activities.

Cataloging-in-Publication Data

Peppas, Lynn.
Terrorism alert! / written by Lynn Peppas.
p. cm. -- (Disaster alert!)
Includes index.
ISBN-13: 978-0-7787-1585-6 (rlb)
ISBN-10: 0-7787-1585-X (rlb)
ISBN-13: 978-0-7787-1617-4 (pbk)
ISBN-10: 0-7787-1617-1 (pbk)
1. Terrorism--Juvenile literature. I. Title. II. Series.
HV6431.P45 2005
303.6'25--dc22

2005019382

LC

Printed in the USA/062017/JF20170515

Published in Canada
Crabtree Publishing
616 Welland Ave.
St. Catharines, ON
L2M 5V6

Published in the United States
Crabtree Publishing
PMB 59051
350 Fifth Avenue, 59th Floor
New York, New York 10118

Published in the United Kingdom
Crabtree Publishing
Maritime House
Basin Road North, Hove
BN41 1WR

Published in Australia
Crabtree Publishing
3 Charles Street
Coburg North
VIC, 3058

Contents

Power and Terror

Terrorism is very difficult to define. Most people agree that terrorism involves acts of violence such as kidnappings, bombings, and hijackings that are carried out by organized groups to gain attention and advance a cause. What people cannot agree on is the justification, or reason, for terrorism.

What is a disaster? A disaster is a destructive event that affects the natural world and human communities. Some disasters are predictable, but others occur without warning. Coping successfully with a disaster depends on a community's preparation.

Violence and victims

Terrorist acts are often violent and secretly planned. They are intended to create fear. Many terrorists believe their acts of violence will force a country or another group of people to change the way they live. They also believe that violent acts are an effective way to promote their ideas or beliefs. The difference between acts of terrorist violence and violence carried out during war is that terrorists often deliberately target innocent victims.

Promoting a cause

Many terrorists have political, religious, or social beliefs they wish to promote. Terrorists believe their acts of violence are the most effective way to bring their message to the public. For example, a terrorist group that believes a government is unjust may try to bomb a government building. The bombing might kill hundreds of people, but the terrorist group would view the bombing as effective because it called attention to its cause and was reported on the news. Terrorists believe that what they are doing is right, even if they kill people.

A man carries an injured child who escaped a terrorist attack at a school in Beslan, Russia, in September 2004.

Secret plans

Terrorism is not new. It has been used by different peoples for thousands of years. An ancient Chinese saying explains that terrorism works to "kill one person to frighten many." Terrorists use many different methods to achieve their goal of making people afraid. It is difficult to recognize terrorists because they work in secrecy and are masters of disguise. Terrorists can be male or female, come from any country in the world, practice any religion, and can be wealthy or poor.

The terrorists who attacked the World Trade Center in New York in 2001 trained in secret.

Ancient assassins

A terrorist who murders a political leader is called an assassin. Assassinations have been happening for thousands of years, but the term assassin did not exist until the year 1092. It is thought that the name assassin was first used in ancient Iran to describe a group of terrorists who murdered people in order to promote a political cause. The original assassins killed princes, military and government officials, and religious leaders who they felt were oppressing them. They always killed their victims with a dagger and were often caught and punished for their crimes. The assassins failed in their main goal of changing society, but the acts of terror they committed are still called assassinations today.

The assassin leader brings new members into his group of terrorists.

Ancient Terrorism

Thousands of years ago, leaders used violence to frighten people who rebelled **against their rule. People who did not obey were tortured or killed to set an example. These rulers used terror to expand and maintain control of their territories.**

Powerful rule

From 1200 B.C. to 625 B.C., ancient Assyria was a powerful **empire** located in present-day Iraq. During their rule, Assyrian kings sent armies to invade and capture surrounding territories. Assyrian soldiers destroyed entire cities. The people they captured were tortured and **impaled** on stakes. These terrifying acts frightened newly **conquered** peoples and discouraged them from openly rebelling against their new rulers.

Roman Empire

Ancient Rome was a powerful empire centered in present-day Italy. Rome had a strong army which conquered many territories, and made them **colonies**. The empire stretched from Turkey to Britain. Over time, the leaders of Rome became very wealthy and powerful. They feared losing their wealth and power so they imprisoned or killed people whose ideas and beliefs differed from their own. Many were killed in acts of terror such as public executions.

Early terrorists used assassination because it targeted one person instead of many. Here, ancient Roman senators are shown assassinating Rome's leader, Julius Caesar, in 44 B.C. The senators believed Caesar was too powerful and would never give up his position as ruler.

Fighting back

Even with the fear of imprisonment and mass **executions**, people found ways to live under their unjust rulers. Some openly resisted their rulers. Rome's emperors demanded high taxes from the people of the areas they ruled. The taxes paid for the emperors' palaces and armies. In 66 A.D., Rome ruled Judea, in present-day Israel, Jordan, and Palestine. Judea was the homeland of the Jews, a people with a long-established religion and culture. When the Roman emperor needed more money, he raided and stole the treasures of the Jewish temple. This upset many Jews who protested and were put to death for it.

The Zealots

One group of Jews, called the Sicarii, or Zealots, resisted Roman rule by raiding the Roman hilltop fort of Masada. The Zealots killed the Roman soldiers there and stole weapons to launch a rebellion called the Jewish Revolt. They fought the Romans and took over the Judean city of Jerusalem. They wanted to rid Judea of Roman rule. The Zealots adopted many of the oppressive tactics of their former rulers, including killing those who did not agree with them. Over time, Jerusalem, and their control over it weakened. The Zealots were forced out of Jerusalem, and took refuge, or shelter, at Masada. The Romans again invaded Judea and laid **siege** to Masada. The Zealots at Masada killed themselves rather than submitting to Roman rule.

The ancient Sicarii, or Zealots, were a group of Jews who resisted Roman rule. The Zealots took over a Roman hilltop fortress called Masada. When the Romans came to take back Masada, the Zealots chose to kill their families and themselves rather than surrender. The word sicarii refers to the daggers that members carried to assassinate people who opposed them. The word zealot is sometimes used today to refer to people who have extreme passions or beliefs.

Reign of Terror

The word terrorism has its roots in the late 1700s in France. At that time, the country was in the middle of a revolution. The king was overthrown by a group of people who wanted to establish a government based on freedom and equality**.**

Revolution!

In 1789, Louis XVI was the king of France. He was a weak ruler, known for his **extravagant** lifestyle. His government was in debt and needed money. Louis XVI tried to raise taxes to cover the debt, but some members of his government wanted to change the way France was run instead. They wanted the people of France to have more say in how they were governed. Fear and food shortages kept the country in **disarray**. A group of people formed a national assembly, which called for a reduction of the king's power. When the king seemed to reject this, an impatient mob in Paris stormed the Bastille jail, where enemies of the king were imprisoned. The mob killed the Bastille's governor and later, the mayor of Paris.

The storming of the Bastille is seen as the beginning of the French Revolution. The revolution began as a revolt against the absolute power of the king and nobility.

New regime

The storming of the Bastille was the beginning of the French Revolution. It signalled a time of change. Rebellions soon began to happen throughout France. The national assembly took power and King Louis XVI and Queen Marie Antoinette were arrested and eventually executed by guillotine, a device that cut off their heads. Laws were made to establish a republic, or government where power rested with the people. Nobles, and other people who did not support the revolution, were jailed and killed.

Terror and turmoil

Over time, the new regime, or government, became a regime of terror. It used terror to frighten people and make them act the way the regime wanted them to. The regime ruled for just one year, but thousands of people were put to death during this time. A new law was passed that allowed the regime to send enemies to the guillotine without proper trials or even a defense for the accused. The regime's aim was to terrorize and get rid of anyone who was thought to oppose it or the revolution.

Robespierre's reign

Maximilien Robespierre was one of the leaders of the French Revolution. He used terror to further the revolution's goals of establishing a free republic to replace the rule of the king, or monarchy. Robespierre was the leader of the Revolution's Reign of Terror from 1793–1794, and was feared by many for his ruthlessness. Robespierre believed the republic was right to use terror to defend freedom, or liberty. He also felt anyone who did not believe what he believed was an enemy and must be killed. His Reign of Terror ended in 1794, when other leaders of the revolution took control and sent him to the guillotine.

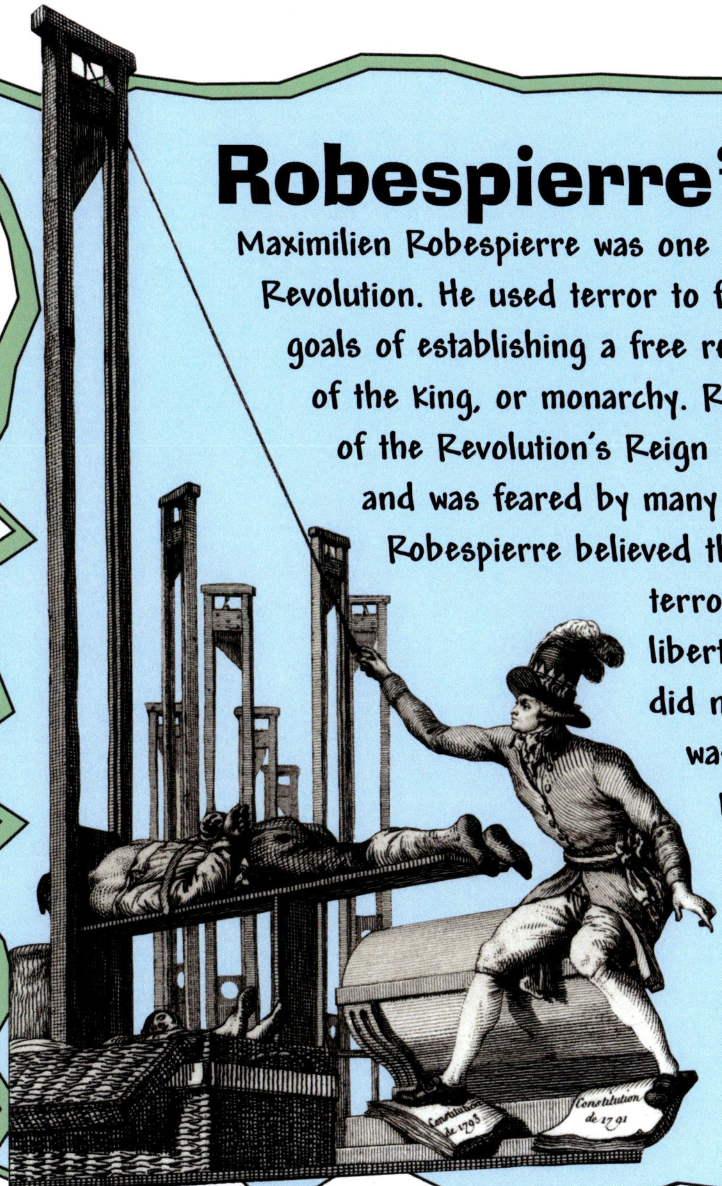

Terror Through Time

Terrorism has been used by many people and groups throughout history, from people fighting to overthrow a government, to governments wanting to frighten and control people. Only the methods and the reasons used by terrorists have changed.

People's Will

One of the first terrorist groups to openly call itself a terrorist group was Narodnaya Volya, or People's Will. Narodnaya Volya began in Russia in 1878. In the late 1800s, Russia was ruled by a tsar, or king, and a government made up mostly of wealthy nobles. Fed up with how Russia treated its peasants and workers, Narodnaya Volya assasinated members of government and the wealthy royalty. Narodnaya Volya chose to assasinate only people in positions of power, such as the tsar. They called off one assassination of a Grand Duke because he was surrounded by his children and they did not want to kill them too. The group succeeded in killing Tsar Alexander II in 1881 by lobbing a bomb at him. Narodnaya Volya was not successful in getting public support for their cause. Eventually, the government hunted down members of the terrorist group, brought them to trial, and executed them.

Igniting a world war

One of the bloodiest wars of the 1900s began as a reaction to an assassination. Franz Ferdinand, the heir to the **Austro-Hungarian Empire**, was shot as he was visiting Bosnia, a territory ruled by the empire. Austria-Hungary declared war on Serbia, a country neighboring Bosnia, because they believed the attack was part of Serbia's plan to free Bosnia so Bosnia and Serbia could unite. Russia, an **ally** of Serbia, then declared war on Austria-Hungary. Many countries that were allied with both sides were pulled into the war.

Police arrest assassin Gavrilo Princip on the street after he shot Archduke Franz Ferdinand and his wife Sophie on June 28, 1914. Princip belonged to Narodna Obrana, a Serbian group that was fighting the rule of the empire. The assassination helped spark World War I.

State terror

The term "state terrorism" refers to acts of terror committed by a country against its citizens. There have been many examples of state terror in history. Often, when countries are accused of acts of terror against their own citizens, their governments deny it. Governments may send armies out to murder all the people in one village or starve entire districts, but the only people who know about these acts are the people doing it and the survivors. Many people believe such mass killings occured in the Soviet Union, a group of **communist** states that broke up in the late 1980s. Some experts estimate that from 1917 to 1987, around 60 million people in the Soviet Union died in labor camps, and through forced starvation and other brutalities inflicted by their governments. Other states are guilty of similar acts of terror. When the mass killing and terror is directed toward citizens of a specific race or ethnic group, it is called genocide.

Human skulls are a grisly reminder of the state terror in Cambodia, a country in Asia. From 1975 to 1978, one million people died in extermination camps set up by their government.

Millions of Soviet citizens were killed in gulags, or prison camps, located in remote places such as northern Siberia.

Anti-Colonial Terrorism

After World War II, many nations struggled to free themselves of rule by foreign governments. Some, such as many African and Asian countries, had been under European colonial rule for decades. The fight to free themselves from this rule and establish independent countries was often violent and bloody. Some anti-colonial groups used violent action to get the attention of the world and their colonial rulers. Anti-colonial terrorist groups used daily or weekly bombings, and assasinations, often in public places, to pressure the foreign government to leave.

(above) The Irish Republican Army, or IRA, was a terrorist group that fought against British rule over Northern Ireland. Thousands of people were killed in decades of violence between the IRA and opposing terrorist groups who supported British rule. Eventually, the IRA and other groups agreed to give up their violent methods.

Terror and Nationalism

The success of some anti-colonial terrorist groups inspired other people fighting for political change. During the 1960s and 1970s many groups used terror to push for independence in countries such as Canada and Spain. In Canada, the Front de Liberation du Quebec, or FLQ carried out bombings, kidnappings, and the killing of a politician in their fight for an independent Quebec.

Mahatma Gandhi

Not all anti-colonial resistance groups used terrorism to fight against their European rulers. Mahatma Gandhi was a spiritual man who fought for an independent India. He believed in a non-violent way of opposing colonialism that involved not cooperating with the rules imposed on Indians by their British rulers. Gandhi said, "Terrorism and deception are weapons not of the strong but of the weak."

Gandhi used non-violent resistance instead of terrorism.

Fighting For A Cause

FLQ members believed that Quebec, a French-speaking province of Canada, should be an independent country. The FLQ's campaign of terror ended in the early 1970s when most of its members were tried for their crimes and jailed. Many Quebecers still believe in the goals of the FLQ, but not the methods. The Freedom for the Basque Homeland group, or ETA, was established in France and Spain in 1959. The ETA used assasinations and bombings in its fight for a separate country for Basques. The Basques are a people who live in northern Spain and southern France. They have a separate language and culture and do not consider themselves French or Spanish. The ETA continues to use bombings to pressure the governments of France and Spain to set up an independent Basque country.

The Palestinian Liberation Organization, or PLO, is a group that formed in 1964 to fight for an independent state of Palestine in territory controlled by Israel in the Middle East. Palestinians and Israelis have fought over the land for many decades. Former Palestinian president Yasser Arafat, was chairman of the PLO. He claimed the use of terror was justified in the fight for a Palestinian country. Over the years, the violence between Israel and Palestine led many people to believe the terror would be endless. Recently, two sides have begun working towards peace and the PLO offically gave up terror as a tactic. Palestinians now have an elected prime minister and the Palestinian authority governs parts of territory claimed by Palestine.

Weapons of Terror

Most terrorists use weapons that are easily carried and concealed, or hidden. Ancient terrorists used daggers, or knives. Modern terrorists depend on high-tech weapons such as guns and explosives that can kill many people at one time.

Today, terrorists train with easy-to-assemble guns such as the AK-47. The AK-47 is a favorite of terrorists because it was designed for use in battle, where soldiers have little time to react. Automatic weapons, such as the AK-47, were designed to shoot many bullets at a time.

Ancient weapons

Ancient peoples did not have powerful weapons such as guns, bombs, and other explosives. Soldiers were armed with swords and knives, and killing was done by hand. Ancient terrorists, including assassins, needed a small but deadly weapon to murder their victims with, and the dagger was a common choice. Daggers are short bladed knives made with stone, flint, animal bone, bronze, jade, or metal. Daggers could be easily hidden in an assassin's clothing.

Crucifixion

Crucifixion was used by governments in ancient times to execute people. The Romans executed criminals, rebels, and those opposed to their rule. Crucifixion was a slow, torturous death in which a victim was nailed or tied to a large wooden cross. Victims often suffered for days and their bodies were left for others to see. Crucifixion was a method of terrorism because it demonstrated to people who were tempted to rebel what would happen to them if they went against their rulers.

Early bombs

Terrorists today use many methods and weapons to carry out attacks and instill fear. In the late 1800s and early 1900s, terrorist groups were small and weapons included guns and bombs. Their targets were often individuals such as presidents, government officials, and members of royalty. Bombs were crudely made with explosives and were often unstable. Still, using bombs proved effective. If they did not accidentally blow up, terrorists could conceal the bombs under clothing and throw them at their targets.

Guns

Pistols and revolvers, or small firearms that are held in one hand, were used by assassins in the 1800s and early 1900s because they could be easily hidden under clothing. United States President Abraham Lincoln was assassinated with a revolver on April 14, 1865. His assassin, John Wilkes Booth, was a **Confederate** sympathizer and a **racist** who did not agree with Lincoln's efforts to end slavery in the United States. After a plan to kidnap Lincoln fell apart, Booth decided to kill the president instead.

John Wilkes Booth shot U.S. President Abraham Lincoln from behind as Lincoln watched a play at Ford's Theater in Washington, D.C., in 1865. He used a revolver because it was small and could easily be hidden under his clothing.

Bombing public spaces

Beginning in the mid-1900s, many terrorist organizations began to choose larger targets in order to bring their messages to a broader public. Instead of lobbing one bomb at a government official, the terrorists began to plant bombs in public gathering places. These bombs killed and maimed many victims and were intended to make everyone feel like they were a target. Terrorists hoped that bombing public places, such as restaurants, theaters, and buses, would make people force their governments into doing what the terrorists wanted in order to stop the bombings.

A crude bomb made from a water container uses a watch as a detonator. Even homemade explosives can kill or maim dozens of people. Today, bombs can be made from plastic explosives that are difficult to detect.

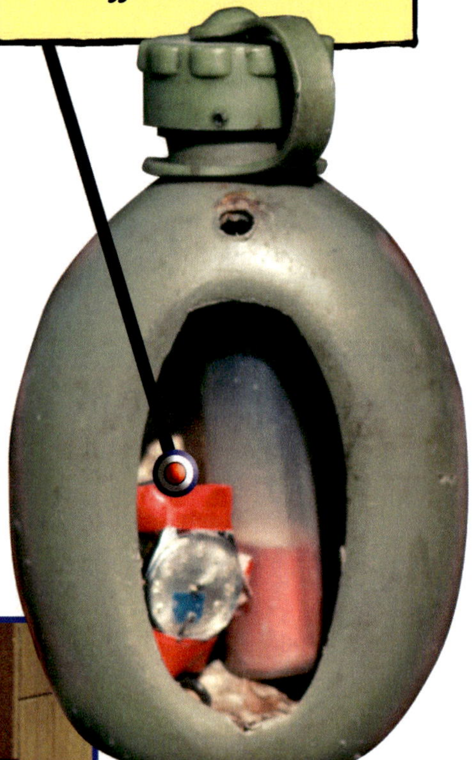

Setting it off

Bombs contain materials that explode when heated or struck. Early explosives were detonated, or set off, by rope fuses. The fuses were set on fire and burned until they reached a **propellant**. Early detonators were unreliable because they did not always ignite the explosives. Modern explosives are much more stable and terrorists today use many different kinds of detonators. Some bombs use clocks as detonators. Cell phones have also been modified and used to set off bombs.

Oklahoma City

American terrorists packed a rental truck with fuel and fertilizer in 1995 and blew it up in front of a government building in Oklahoma. The blast killed 168 people and injured about 800.

Letter bombs

Letter bombs were used by terrorists beginning in the 1940s to target specific victims. Letter bombs are explosives planted in an envelope and then mailed to a person. They were effective because of their size. A letter bomber terrorized Americans for 17 years. Theodore Kaczynski, nicknamed the Unabomber, sent deadly letter bombs through the United States Postal Service. Kaczynski was an unusual terrorist because he acted alone. He felt that new technology was destroying the environment and sent letter bombs to people who were using or creating this technology. His bombs killed three people and injured 23 others. Kaczynski was captured in April, 1996 and after a trial was sentenced to life in prison.

Hijacking and hostage-taking

Hijacking is the violent takeover of a car, bus, or aircraft by terrorists. Most hijackers also take hostages, or people held against their will. Aircraft hijacking became a common form of terrorism in the 1960s and 1970s. Hijackers often negotiated with police and governments for money, their escape from a country, or the release of prisoners who supported their cause. Hijackers threatened to destroy aircraft, either by detonating a bomb aboard the plane or by crashing it into a populated area. There are fewer aircraft hijackings today because better airport security means people cannot sneak weapons aboard a flight. Governments are also less likely to negotiate with hijackers.

Hijackers took over this Air France jet.

The Terror Group

There are hundreds of different terrorist organizations throughout the world today. Each group has different aims and beliefs. People who join terrorist groups support those aims and are willing to injure and kill others to carry them out.

Using terror

A terrorist group is an organization that uses terror to achieve its goals. Sometimes the goals are to force a **foreign occupier** out of a territory they have claimed. Other times it is to change the way a country is governed. Terrorist acts such as bombings and kidnappings are meant to draw attention to the goals of the group, and to frighten people. Terrorists hope governments will take action, or meet their goals in order to end the fear.

In 1974, Patty Hearst, a wealthy heiress, was kidnapped by a group of American terrorists known as the Symbionese Liberation Army, or SLA. The SLA was opposed to people with money and power. After her kidnapping, Hearst participated in terrorist acts with the group. When caught she said she was brainwashed into joining the SLA.

Leadership and funding

Some terrorists act alone but most are members of groups. Terrorist groups have stated goals and their members work together. Many terrorist groups have leaders who plan actions and find the money to carry them out. This money comes from a number of sources, including donations from people or governments who believe in the group's goals. Terrorists have also robbed banks to fund their organizations.

Women guerrilla fighters of the Liberation Tigers of Tamil Eelam (LTTE), in Sri Lanka, wear military uniforms. The Tamil Tigers are a group that carries out terrorist acts while fighting for an independent country.

What's in a name?

In the late 1800s, members of the Russian terrorist group Narodnaya Volya openly admitted to being terrorists. Today, terrorists rarely call themselves terrorists. Instead, they choose names that describe their goals or tactics. Here are some names and their meanings:

* Extremist: A person who strongly believes in an idea.
* Guerrillas: A small band of fighters who use surprise attacks during conflicts. From the Spanish word guerra, or war.
* Freedom fighter: A person who takes part in armed rebellion or resistance against a government that he or she feels is overly harsh or oppressive.
* Insurgent: Someone who rises in revolt, often violently, against a government or authority.
* Rebel: Someone who resists or defies authority.
* Revolutionary: Someone who supports the overthrow of a government and its replacement with another.
* Militant: Someone who fights and belongs to a group that organizes itself like an army.
* Fundamentalist: Someone who strictly follows their religious views.
* Radical: A person whose beliefs go against the accepted beliefs.
* Fanatic: A person with extreme, unreasoning enthusiasm for a cause.
* Zealot: Someone who is extremely enthusiastic about a cause.

The State and Terror

Sometimes the government of a country commits acts of terror against its own people. This is called state terrorism. One of the most violent examples of state terrorism was that of the Nazi regime in Germany from 1933 to 1945.

Nazi power

The Nazi regime was a government in Germany prior to and during **World War II**. Under the leadership of **dictator** Adolf Hitler, the Nazis used terror to control the German people and people of many other countries that they occupied, or took over, during the war. The Nazis were racist and believed that the German people were a race, or group of people, **superior** to all others. They threatened or eliminated anyone who opposed their rule or who did not agree with their beliefs. In power, Hitler and the Nazis also banned all other political parties so that there would be no government opposition to their rule.

The Hitler Youth was a Nazi group set up to train German children in Nazi ideas. At weekly meetings and rallies, members were taught to exercise, to use weapons, and to believe what the Nazi Party told them to believe. Children were taught to hate Jews and other people hated by the Nazis. By 1936, a law was passed forcing all German children to join the group.

A street in Berlin, Germany, with the shattered fronts of Jewish-owned stores. On the night of November 9, 1938, the Nazis organized Kristallnacht, or Night of the Broken Glass, where Germans terrorized the Jews of Germany, killing over 100, and sending thousands to camps.

Nazi terror

In the 1930s, Germany, like many other countries, suffered during an international economic crisis called the Great Depression. Hitler blamed Germany's hardships, including massive **unemployment**, on the country's Jews and other people. The Nazis set about terrorizing those people. Jews lost their rights and could not vote, inherit land, or travel freely. They were attacked in the streets. Jews, along with many others who the Nazis hated, were forced into **concentration camps** where they worked as slave laborers, or were tortured, then killed.

After the war, Allied soldiers found concentration camps full of dead and half-starved victims of Nazi terror. Millions of people died in these camps and the memory of the terror lived on for survivors.

War and terror

During World War II, Nazi Germany took over and occupied many European countries. Over six years, the Nazi regime murdered six million Jews in an organized system of extermination. The regime was crushed in 1945 after years of war against the Allies, which included the United States, Canada, Britain, and the Soviet Union. German leader Adolf Hitler committed suicide. Other Nazi leaders were tried, convicted, and sentenced for war crimes instead of acts of terror.

A Terrorizing Triumph

Following World War II, terrorism was used by some groups in their struggles to free their countries from colonial rule. In the North African country of Algeria, the fight to be free of French rule was one of the bloodiest in history.

(above) France colonized Algeria and gained power over the people who lived there with the help of its powerful army.

French rule

France began to send settlers, called *colons*, to Algeria in 1830. The *colons* set up a colonial government and took over the best land to farm. They made Algerians second-class, or inferior, citizens in their own country. Algerians had to carry **permits** with them when they wanted to travel through their own country. The only jobs available to Algerians usually required a lot of hard, physical labor, such as working on a *colon*'s farm for very little money. The Algerians began to resent the French *colons* and over time, some decided to fight the *colons*, force them out, and establish an independent country.

War of independence

In 1954, a group called the Front de libération nationale, or FLN, declared war on French rule. They demanded that the French government hand over control of Algeria. The FLN began a campaign of terror by targeting French military and government sites. Soon after, they began targeting civilians and tourists. The French Army responded with even greater acts of violence against Algerians, including mass murders and torture. Thousands of innocent people were injured or killed during this time.

(below) After eight years of fighting, Algerian FLN members cry as their country is set free from 132 years of French rule.

Independence

People outside of Algeria, including many citizens of France, were outraged at the brutal means the army was using to fight the FLN and believed France should withdraw from Algeria. In 1962, under pressure from its own citizens and from many other countries around the world, France granted Algeria its independence. The FLN took control of the government, and went from terrorist group to political party. The majority of *colons* did not stay in Algeria. Since then, Algerians have gone through more hard times, including a **civil war**. Once in power and fearing competition from religious parties, the FLN refused to allow other parties to run against it in elections. This led to more terrorism from groups opposed to the FLN-led government.

Terrorists blew up a building in Rouiba, Algeria, in 1995. Algeria did not immediately heal from its bloody fight for independence and an uneasy peace has only recently come to the country.

Women in battle

As the number of attacks by the FLN increased, the French began to suspect that most Algerian men were terrorists. Men were watched very carefully, making it difficult for the FLN to carry out its plans. In September 1956, three female FLN members planted bombs in a café, a milk bar, and the headquarters of a French airline, in the capital city of Algiers. Dozens of people were injured or killed when the bombs exploded. This marked the beginning of the Battle of Algiers, an eight-month attack designed by the FLN to attract attention to their cause.

Women members of the FLN planted bombs and brought food to men fighting in the streets.

Training for Terror

Terrorists train for action in secret. Some attend hidden training camps where they are taught to make and use weapons. Others learn how to make bombs from books and manuals.

Mikhail Kalashnikov is the Russian soldier who built the Kalashnikov or AK-47 assault rifle in 1947. He worked on the gun's design while recovering from wounds received during World War II. Today, the AK-47 is the world's most widely-used weapon for armies and for terrorists.

Recruiting terrorists

Terrorist groups recruit, or bring in, new members in a number of ways. Sometimes people believe in the goals of a terrorist group and are persuaded to join. They believe terrorism is the best way to take action against oppression because they think that they are victims or are fighting on behalf of victims. Terrorist groups also recruit by using propaganda that describes their group or their goals as good. Propaganda is the use of speeches, media, movies, music, or even religious books that promote the ideals or causes of a group or organization.

Books and the Internet

Some terrorist organizations share training information, such as books, with other terrorist organizations with similar beliefs and aims. *The Minimanual of the Urban Guerrilla*, written by a South American revolutionary was copied and given to members of a German terrorist group in the 1970s. Manuals like these explain things such as the importance of physical fitness, fighting techniques, weapon building and operations, and how to keep plans for violent acts a secret. Today, terrorists can also learn how to make a bomb from everyday household items, or forge an **identity document** by reading books or searching the Internet.

Off to camp

It is difficult to know the exact locations of terrorist training camps because they operate in secrecy. Much of the information gathered on them is from captured terrorists. Experts do know that terrorists sent to training camps are taught how to launch an attack and what to do if they are caught. Terrorist camps are hidden in remote areas of the world, and look from the outside like farms or businesses.

(below) Terrorists train for armed combat by crawling under barbed wire and jumping over pits.

William Powell wrote The Anarchist Cookbook as an angry student in 1970. The book included recipes for making crude bombs. Powell has since changed his views on violent action and has tried to get the book's publisher to stop printing it. Critics say the book's recipes are not used by real terrorists, who use more sophisticated weapons and arguments in their battles.

Baghdad, Iraq

Terror on the Ground

The secrecy in which terrorists operate makes it difficult to know when and where a terrorist attack will occur. Deadly attacks have happened in almost every country in the world. All terrorist attacks are planned to spread fear.

Media coverage

Terrorist attacks are planned to have the most impact and attract the most attention. If the act is reported on television or in newspapers, the terrorists feel more people will know about their cause. Sometimes the public is so horrified by the act that the terrorists only make people hate them and not understand their cause.

A terror attack on a school in Russia killed 340 people. The terrorists took hostages and did not allow them food, water, or sleep for three days.

Beslan hostage-taking

On September 1, 2004, terrorists raided a school in Beslan, Russia, taking 1,200 children, parents, and teachers as hostages. The hostages were held in the school gym. The terrorists were from a group demanding the independence of Chechnya, a part of Russia. Russian troops had been fighting Chechens since 1995, in a war that killed thousands. After three days, a gun battle broke out between Russian Security Service officers and the terrorists. Over 340 people were killed in the school by bombs and guns.

In 1995, members of a religious group called Aum Shinrikyo, or Supreme Truth, released a deadly chemical called sarin gas in the Tokyo subway system during rush hour. The terrorist attack killed 12 people, and injured thousands of others. Japanese police officers later arrested the group's leader and 40 members and charged them with murder.

Munich Massacre

Terrorists sometimes use public events to launch attacks. Knowing the world would be watching, a Palestinian terrorist group called The Black September Organization launched an attack on athletes from Israel at the September 1972 Olympic Games in Munich, Germany. Eight Black September terrorists entered the Olympic compound and killed two Israeli athletes, and kidnapped nine others. Black September demanded the release of 232 Palestinians that were in Israeli jails. Unprepared for a terrorist attack, German police bungled a later rescue attempt and the hijackers killed the rest of their hostages. Five of the eight terrorists were also killed in a gunfight, along with a German police officer. Olympic events continued throughout the massacre. The attack made the world take notice and security forces in Europe began to train for terrorist attacks.

Protesters carry a poster with the names of the athletes killed by terrorists at the 1972 Olympics. They wanted the people who planned the attack to be charged.

Terror in the Sky

Commercial **aircraft became popular targets for terrorist attacks beginning in the 1960s. Terrorists took advantage of lax airport security at the time and brought weapons aboard flights. Hijacking aircraft became a sure way to make people afraid to fly and bring attention to a terrorist cause.**

Airport security

Airports in many parts of the world used to have relaxed security. In the 1960s, passengers and luggage boarded planes without being searched. There were no metal detectors, meaning terrorists could board flights with **concealed** weapons and bombs. When terrorists began hijacking planes, airports and airlines began to follow strict rules aimed at stopping hijackers before the gate. In 1970, armed sky marshals were put on selected flights in the United States. The marshals were responsible for protecting passengers from gun-toting terrorists on flights, but they could not be aboard every flight.

Baggage check

By 1972 in the United States, the Federal Aviation Administration, the organization that **regulated** airlines, asked all airlines to check passengers and baggage. Other countries soon did the same. The metal detectors used today are so sensitive that they can detect change in pockets and tweezers in carry-on bags. When terrorists began putting bombs in luggage, airports and airlines began checking all luggage, including portable computers and electronic equipment to make sure they were not packed with explosives.

A Royal Canadian Mounted Police officer guards the wreckage of Air India Flight 182. The wreckage was pulled from the ocean near Ireland after the plane blew up in 1985. Terrorists planted a bomb in a piece of luggage that killed 329 people. Twenty years after the bombing, two men were tried for the bombing. One man was acquitted for lack of evidence, which left the families of the victims frustrated and hurt.

New York City, U.S.A

Hijackings

Many early terrorist hijackings ended when governments gave in to terrorist demands. The earliest hijacking, or skyjacking, of a commercial airplane happened in 1948. Hijacking was a favorite tactic of **revolutionary** terrorists in the 1960s. They often asked to be flown to countries that accepted their politics, or they asked that **comrades** be set free from jail in return for hostages. In 1970, terrorists from several Palestinian organizations began hijacking planes. The terrorists wanted Palestine, a region of the Middle East occupied in part by Israel, to become an independent country. The terrorists, from the Popular Front for the Liberation of Palestine, hijacked three planes and destroyed them after the hostages were taken off the flights. On another hijacked plane, a terrorist was killed and another was captured. Other terrorists threatened to kill their hostages if the hijacker was not released. Their demands were met and hijacking became more popular. When airport security improved, hijackings became more difficult. Terrorists could no longer board a plane with concealed guns and bombs.

On September 11, 2001, 19 terrorists from the al-Qaeda group hijacked four airplanes, using box-cutter knives as weapons. The terrorists, who were trained to fly, took control and flew two aircraft into New York's World Trade Center. Other aircraft were flown into the Pentagon, and into a field in Pennsylvania. The attacks killed at least 2,985 people, including people on the flights, in the buildings, and on the ground. The United States launched a "War on Terror" after the attacks in an attempt to stop terrorists before they attacked again.

Fighting Terrorism

Counter-terrorism is a government's effort to prevent acts of terrorism through security agencies and special police and military forces. Counter-terrorists gather information, or intelligence, about terrorist organizations.

Gathering intelligence

Security, or intelligence agencies, such as the Central Intelligence Agency, or CIA, in the United States, collect information on suspected terrorists and terrorist groups. They share that information, which includes satellite photos of terrorist training camps, and information on the location of terrorists, with other security and intelligence groups throughout the world. They do this to learn how the groups operate, who their members are, and how they might be stopped.

(above) An anti-terrorist squad practices repelling down a building.

Eye see you

At terrorist targets such as skyscrapers and crowded stadiums, security personnel are trained to watch large crowds of people. **Surveillance** cameras scan faces in the crowd and match them with photos of suspected terrorists in a computer database. Some buildings require visitors to pass through metal detectors and security checkpoints to ensure that they are not carrying weapons.

Armed response

Counter-terrorism rescue units respond quickly in emergencies to diffuse bombs or rescue hostages. Many counter-terrorism units are specialized units of the military or police. Members are trained as snipers, and they are taught how to dispose of bombs, and to negotiate for the release of hostages. Their goal is to save lives and prevent terrorists from acting again.

(below) A visitor has her fingerprint taken at an airport as part of a program that screens foreign travelers to prevent known terrorists from entering the U.S.

Security or freedom?

Governments take action against terrorist threats and acts of violence by creating laws that allow their security forces to arrest, hold in jail, and **prosecute** terrorists and even people thought to be terrorists. In 2001, Britain updated its anti-terrorism laws and allowed police and other government agencies more power to investigate and hold suspected terrorists as prisoners. Many other countries, including Canada, have passed laws to defend against terrorism since September 11, 2001. In the United States, the Department of Homeland Security was created in 2001 to prevent and respond to terrorist threats. Many people believe firm laws will keep them safe from terrorists, while others say that restricting freedoms, such as holding people in jail for indefinite periods of time, is wrong because it takes away people's rights.

Israel built an enormous wall to protect its citizens from terrorist acts. Critics argue that the wall will only anger people, especially those whose land it was built on, and increase acts of terrorism.

Glossary

ally A partner
anarchist A person who believes and promotes the idea that government is not necessary
Austro-Hungarian Empire A group of countries in Eastern Europe including Hungary and Austria that joined together from 1867 to 1918
civil war A war fought between people from the same country
colony An area that is ruled by another country
commercial For profit or gain
communist A system of governing in which all services are controlled by the government
comrades People who belong to the same organization and share the same ideas
conceal To hide
concentration camp A prison camp used to hold political prisoners during a war
Confederate A person that belonged to a group of 11 Southern States in the 1860s that separated from the United States and agreed with slavery
conquer To take over by force
dictator A leader who has sole and complete control over a country
disarray Confusion or disorder
empire A group of countries or areas that are all ruled by the same leader
equality Having the same amount of something, such as rights
execution Put to death
extravagant Beyond what is necessary
foreign occupier A government or armed group that has taken over rule of another country
identity document An official piece of paper that shows who you are
impale To kill on a sharp point or pole
nobility People with power to rule, usually because of wealth or family status
oppress To put down or cause to suffer
permits Permission that has been given in the form of a written document
propellant A substance that creates a forward or outward moving force
prosecute To take legal action against a suspected criminal
racist A person who dislikes others because of their culture or skin color
rebel To fight against a government or leader
regulate To make rules that must be followed
revolutionary A person or action that fights for a change in government or leader
siege To surround an area with the goal of taking control of it
sophisticated Advanced
superior Better
surveillance To carefully watch something
unemployment Without enough work
World War II An international conflict that lasted from 1939 to 1945

Index